ROUND
TRIP
ANN JONAS

Round Trip

Library of Congress Cataloging in
Publication Data
Jonas, Ann. Round trip.
"Greenwillow Books."
Summary: Black and white illustrations and
text record the sights on a day trip to the city
and back home again to the country.
[1. Cities and towns—Fiction.
2. Country life—Fiction.]
I. Title.
PZ7.J664Ro 1983   [E]   82-12026
ISBN 0-688-01772-X (trade)
ISBN 0-688-01781-9 (lib. bdg.)
ISBN 0-688-09986-6 (pbk.)

First Edition

30 29 28 27 26 25 24 23 22

For Don, Nina, Amy

We started out as soon as it was light.

Our neighborhood was quiet, the houses dark.

Town was empty,
the stores still closed.

We passed a small farm in the valley,

and fields of wheat.
We counted the cars on a train.

It rained hard
and puddles formed.

The road wound through the mountains.
Trails led into the woods.

Lightning flashed across the sky.

On the highway,
we headed for the coast.

We went under an expressway.

The water was rough, the waves high.

As the smoke from the fireworks drifted away
and the birds resettled in the trees, we drove on.

We followed the shore past marshy inlets

We saw fireworks and stopped to watch.

Then we saw the city.

We looked back. Searchlights pierced the sky.

We crossed a bridge,

In the country, telephone poles lined the road.

and we were there.

We left the shining, starlit city.

After parking the car, we rode the subway.

and picked up our car from the garage.

Then we went to a movie,

Then we had dinner in a restaurant,

and to the top of the tallest building.
We looked down.

Back on the street,
we looked up at where we had been.

The sky was dark.
Lights came on all over the city.

We watched as the sun set.
Time to turn around.